Rampage at Redd Ranch

- Or -

The Satanic Samaritans

By An Old Deputy

Rampage at Redd Ranch

- Or -

The Satanic Samaritans
By An Old Deputy

Foreword

Hello Dear Reader,

The book you hold is a prequel to my horror adventure novel, Life Is In The Blood. This excursion into that world features one of its protagonists. The hard as nails and surly lawman of Sikeston, Missouri, Sheriff Flynn.

This dime novel of West of Weird Weekly chronicles the first encounter of Sheriff Flynn with Silas Hemfant and the Samaritans. Its told in the style of the Western novels of the 1890s. So, get your horse ready, your six-shooters and prepare to ride out against some nasty hombres.

Be sure to subscribe to my newsletter at DanielBautzCTP.com to get a FREE copy of the companion prequel, The Haunting of McMurtry Manor.

Of course, don't miss out on the start of a grand adventure, Life Is In The Blood, available on Amazon.com.

Thanks for reading,
Daniel Bautz

Rampage at Redd Ranch

- Or -

The Satanic Samaritans

Chapter One - Sheriff Flynn Draws the Line

"Don't mess with a man's livestock. That's messing with his life and your own."

The speaker was a tall, raw-boned, muscular black man in his late forties. The sheriff of Sikeston wasn't one to waste words or be trifled with. He rode against Lincoln's men in the war, clawed his way to freedom, and fought his way to becoming a respected lawman in this wild frontier town.

His imposing frame was covered in the typical ware of the western highwayman. Denim pants under leather riding chaps, brown leather boots spurred with bronze, a dark brown ten-gallon hat, a red handkerchief tied around his neck, and a blue cotton shirt with a bronze star hanging over his left breast. A leather holster held his pistol against his left outer thigh. His thick mustache covered his top lip, but my guess is it seldom hid a smile.

Observing him from a distance, he was not one you would hope to have a quarrel with. In fact, keeping your space seemed a wisdom for most.

The scene was at the Redd Ranch. A nice swatch of farmland a few miles from town. Our sheriff stood where the wagon trail leading to the house and barn met the dirt road. It was his duty, but it was clear Sheriff Flynn would rather be elsewhere.

"Proof, Sheriff," The pale, tall, slender man in the black planter's hat said. "Accusations are cheap. Do you have any proof?"

The man was not the rightful owner of the land, at least not in the estimation of our sheriff. But he was the man that came out to meet us. The sheriff rested his left hand on the handle of his pistol, his thumb tapping at the hammer. "I didn't come out here to speak with you. This ain't your land. This is Redd Ranch."

"It is my home. It is mine. You already had this discussion with Ambrose. And I don't think it bears repeating."

"Get Ambrose out here. Now." Sheriff Flynn's thumb tapped the hammer of his pistol faster and faster. His amber eyes narrowed to slits. You could hear him suck at his teeth. Like a coiled rattler, he was ready to strike at the narrow man in the black hat.

"He doesn't want to speak with you, and you have no legal recourse." The man stepped toward the Sikeston sheriff.

"No legal recourse? I am the law, you smug varmint." Sheriff Flynn stepped toward the man squatting at Redd Ranch.

"You don't, and you have even less than you think. So, unless you have a warrant or some proof of the livestock rustling you accused us of, leave." The man smiled. His dark eyes sparkled in the bright midday sun. The man turned his back to the sheriff.

Sometimes, a man needs to do what he must. The sheriff grabbed the arm of the tall man. The man twisted and struck the sheriff in his chest, knocking him back a few feet.

That was it. The pistol flashed from the holster, and the hammer clicked into an open position. The preacher's smile grew as he stared into the barrel of the sheriff's iron.

"I am ready to meet the maker, sheriff. So go ahead and shoot. It will only make me a martyr and you an outlaw."

The sheriff's middle finger twitched inside the trigger guard. His eyes never shifted from the target. The migrant preacher, who came to town months before, showed no fear. He stared at the man and the raised gun without tension.

"Flynn, stop!" The man who yelled came out onto the porch of the house up the wagon wheel trail. Flynn's eyes shifted from the tall man to the one running down the lane toward him.

"Consarn it, Ambrose! I aim to shoot this man, and there's not much words can do 'bout that." Flynn said, his outstretched arm still pointing his pistol at the unconcerned man.

"Put it down. Brother Silas has every right to be here. Moreso than you." The man from the porch stepped in front of the aimed weapon. "Flynn, lower it. I can't have you spilling his blood."

"Step aside, Ambrose." Flynn gritted his teeth. "I don't want to shoot you, but I've got a job to do. Him and his followers are cattle rustlers."

Ambrose, a typical farmer, strong, thin, dirty, and dressed in coveralls with a beat-up flat-brimmed hat, laughed at the words of Sikeston's sheriff. "Flynn, Brother Silas is no more a cattle rustler than you are Jefferson Davis. Tell him, Silas, you're a man of God."

"That is true. I bring the miracle of salvation to all with ears to hear. I am no devil but a simple man of God." Silas offered at the request of Ambrose.

The sheriff's thumb drew back the hammer of his pistol and gently returned it to rest. He dropped his arm. "Ambrose Redd, tell me you ain't falling for this hornswoggler's hogwash."

Ambrose Redd shook his head. "It's not hogwash. You should really listen to him and open your heart to his message, Flynn."

"He's speaks the truth, Sheriff Flynn."

"You shut up! I don't need no guff from you!" Flynn holstered his pistol, grabbed his hat from his head, and wiped the sweat from his brow. "Ambrose, what are you doing? This sidewinder is nothing but trouble, and you're hitching yourself to it."

"You've got it all wrong. He's not trouble unless you want to be a part of the world. He offers hope."

Flynn put his hat back on. "You know, you and your girls, family to me. But I can't side with no cattle thieves, and if you're putting yourself in part with them, I'm not going to have a choice. I don't want to see my brother dangling from no rope."

"We aren't cattle thieves." The preacher spoke up.

"Shut your mouth, or I will shut it for you. This is a family matter."

"Ambrose is my family now." The preacher seemed to have more spine than most. Flynn often found all he needed was a stern word, and most gave themselves over to want he said.

Flynn ignored the preacher. Flynn spit on the ground, whistled, and his horse came up beside him. "Pull out this tick and get him and his horde to get moving on, Ambrose."

Ambrose shook his head. "Flynn, it doesn't have to be like this. Silas and his Samaritans are a good thing. For my family, my farm, and this town."

"Good for you? The farm? How many head of cattle you got right now? Ain't you sign over the deed to the farm to him? Not your farm, it's his."

"Store up your treasures in Heaven." Ambrose retorted. He knew all his cattle were gone.

"Ambrose, we fought side by side for the south. You know what we done. Ain't no Heaven waiting for us."

Chapter Two – Samuel Lee's Fiery Farm

Samuel Lee poured water on his coarse hands to wash the dirt from them before dinner. Annabelle, his wife, stood at the fireplace, ready to pull the cornbread from the pan. Their seven children surrounded the plain table in their small farmhouse.

Samuel watched the water turn to mud and opened his front door to throw out the filthy water. He was greeted with the mooing of his cows. In the darkened edge of twilight, he could see several shadows running from his barn, followed by his cattle.

Cattle thieves!

Samuel fought his instinct to yell at the men leading his cows from his barn. Instead, he backed into his house and pressed the door shut with careful attention not to make noise. He raised his finger over his lips as he faced his family at the dinner table. With his hands, he signaled for everyone to get under the table. He called to his eldest child, "Get to town. Get the sheriff. Go out back."

The eldest child climbed out the window at the back of the house. Once the rest of his family hid under the table, he grabbed his Spencer repeating rifle from its place on the mantle. He checked his ammunition as he snuck to the front windows by his door. He had seven rounds loaded but no clue how many robbers were stealing his livestock. He cocked the lever to place the first round into the breech.

Samuel almost crashed the barrel through the glass of his own window but remembered how much he paid for it. He slid open the window enough to slide his barrel out and sight the marauders. He leaned his cheek to his shoulder, closed his left eye, and centered the bead of his sight on the shadow of a bandit. Samuel drew in a deep breath, held it, and squeezed the trigger.

With a loud bang, the rifle barrel flashed and kicked up against the window sash, shattering the glass. Samuel's wife and children screamed with their fingers in their ears. None of that mattered to Samuel. He heard the cattle thieves screaming. His aim was true. But now they knew they had been discovered.

Samuel quickly tried to aim again, but his targets were hidden among the animals. He thought he saw a head pop up by his bull. He shot. His prize heffer dropped. He heard all kinds of cussing and then heard breaking glass.

The night went from shades of navy to brilliant orange. Flames climbed the dried wooden outer walls of Samuel's barn. He could hear his trusty steed screaming in his stable. The sound made a tear roll down the cheek of Samuel, and murder boiled over inside. With five rounds still in the chamber and his barn alight, Samuel stormed outside.

He spotted several men with his cattle. His rifle shot again, again, again, again, again. Samuel wasn't sure if he hit anything in the smokey night.

With his barn engulfed, Samuel lowered his rifle. The heat of the inferno swirled around him. There was no saving the barn, but at least his family was safe. And his horse suffered no longer. Poor girl. He would fetch Sheriff Flynn, and together, they'd track the cattle down. That's why they were branded.

He was sure the dastardly plunderers hid among his stolen livestock. Samuel was wrong. Not all the thieves ran away. One stood on his porch. Dressed in black with a black planter's hat, the lithe man stood hand clasped together.

"You killed one of mine," the man said.

"Dang right, I did, and you're next." Samuel raised, cocked, aimed, and dry-fired the rifle in a breath.

"I don't think so. And you will pay for that." The man laughed, and he walked into the house. Samuel threw his rifle in the dirt and raced inside.

The man in black tossed over the table Samuel's family hid under. He grabbed Annabelle by her hair, lifting her to her feet. "This sow is a good start, and her litter will be a nice treat. My followers will be happy to use their gifts."

"Get away from my family," Samuel shouted at the man.

"Sorry, but I came for blood," the man said. Samuel charged the intruder. "And cattle only do so much."

Samuel crashed into the man. The two slammed against the table. Children scattered to the corners of the farmhouse as the men tumbled onto the wooden floor. Fists flew like the hammers that drove the railway west.

Back and forth, the men rolled across the planks of the floor and onto the hearth of the fireplace. The intruder snatched an iron poker up. He rose to his feet. Samuel, looking up from his back, watched the blackened iron crash into his face. Teeth splintered, nose twisted, and the skin on Samuel Lee's forehead ripped open.

Annabelle, screaming like a hyena, jumped on the back of the stranger to prevent the killing blow. Her nails streamed over the supple flesh of his face. The scream shifted from pain to rage. The bellow was a portend of the violence about to erupt from the cattle rustler. The metal poker stabbed into the open mouth, rending the jagged teeth of Samuel into his now bloody gullet.

Annabelle bit the ear of the attacker. Underneath, her fingernails filled with the flesh of the intruding murderous maniac as she used them like the claws of a wild mountain lion. The man lurched forward, colliding against the mantle of the fireplace. Annabelle continued to rend, rip, and rupture the attacker's skin with her claws and teeth.

"Enough!" The man grabbed at the paroxysmal woman on his back as she continued to assault him. He caught hold of her long braid and whipped her from his back. She swung like a weight on a pendulum and hurtled into her husband, Samuel. The wife and husband, mother and father, lay in a heaving mass of humanity before the bleeding and slashed thief in the night.

With a boot heel, he calmed the mighty mite of a woman. One swift kick and the fight ended. He ran a finger over the deep grooves in his face, looked at the blood on his digit, and sucked it from his hand. He shook his head. "You just had to fight back. If you'd just let us take the cows..."

He was interrupted by a faint thump against his backside. He looked over his shoulder to see a tow-headed child, fists clenched and staring back at him. A smile crept over the man's face.

The cattle thief stood as he tossed the last parcel into the wagon he rode to the Lee Farm in and stretched his back. He pulled a cloth from his pocket and wiped the soot from his face. The white of his eyes glowed as he looked back at the towering flames that swallowed the farmhouse and barn of Samuel Lee.

Chapter Three – Tussle In Town

Sheriff Flynn felt sick. There was nothing to be done. Samuel Lee and his family were gone, his cattle snatched, and the barn and house nothing but embers and cinder. Orphaned, James Lee could only hope for justice. And by Hell or high water, Sheriff Flynn was going to get him just that.

Sheriff Flynn didn't like the fact that livestock was being snatched and the thieves were still far from hanging. James Lee didn't give him much to go on. But Flynn was already certain. He just needed to catch the no-good crooks with the cows. The brand would seal the deal, and then the sheriff would see that smug evangelist swinging.

Mayor Shelby made the sad blunder of thinking it was his place to motivate the sheriff to get justice. The boards of the porch of the sheriff's shack groaned beneath the burden of Mayor Shelby as he pounded on Flynn's door.

The door swung open, "You better watch your tone, mayor. Coffee's still brewing, and I didn't get a heap of sleep last night."

"I'm sure you know that the town is on the edge of lawlessness, and there's a mob brewing ready to ride out to the Redd homestead?" The mayor was careful not to make the accusation that the townsfolk came to him with.

"Yeah, I know. And they, your mob, do they know how I handle their brand of justice?" Flynn poured coffee into his metal cup and sighed as he sipped.

"And how is that? How do you handle mob justice?"

Flynn looked the mayor in his eye as he took a draw of his coffee. "Same way I handle cattle thieves."

The mayor raised an eyebrow, and his lip quivered as if waiting to ask a question.

Flynn swallowed more coffee and spoke. "Let me save you that question. I will either ventilate their brainpan or stretch their necks. Got no need for a thief or a cowhand playing law."

"You can't just shoot citizens." Mayor Shelby didn't like the sound of his voters dying.

"But I can put down a dirty outlaw when I come across them. So, if some dung shoveler thinks he has a right to take the law into their hands, they are criminals, and last time I checked, I wear the star." Sheriff Flynn made a gun with his hand by extending his index finger up to Mayor Shelby's nose and his thumb toward the roof of his porch. He dropped his thumb. "Bang. No more outlaws. Clear?"

"I understand. Well, then you need to fix this and quick because the fuse is lit, and it's burning right toward the powder keg." Mayor Shelby backed away and stumbled down the steps from the porch. "You need to fix this."

"You need to keep your voters in check, or my deputies and I will take care of your next election. Keep the lid on it, follow?"

"You do your part, Flynn. I will do mine."

Sheriff Flynn finished his coffee and buckled his belt around his waist. Time to wrangle up his deputies and ride out to the Redd Ranch. He looked out the window of his shack as the plump mayor waddled down the street toward his favorite drinking hole, the saloon at the Central Hotel. "Fat pig."

Sheriff Flynn put on his hat and stepped out into the thoroughfare in front of his humble home. He headed south on Front Street. His deputies no doubt filled their bellies at the Central Hotel.

The sheriff was briny and didn't tip his hat back to none of the townsfolk as they passed by. Suppose the mayor's visit had a touch to do with that. Not to mention his best friend falling in with the darn preacher and his Samaritans and the trouble boiling over there. Can't imagine that would soften any man's demeanor.

Problems come in three, they say.

Here was one. On his way to fetch his subordinates, Flynn was greeted with a smile and outstretched hand by that evangelist what swept into town and was putting two old partners at odds.

"You stupid or something?" Flynn squinted and spit at the dirt between the two of them.

"No."

"You must be. But you saved me the pain of riding out to snatch your mangy hide. Much obliged." Flynn began to pull his iron from his belt.

"Snatch. For what?" The man did his best to play shocked, but our sheriff wasn't buying.

"The destruction of Lee Homestead and stealing his cattle. So, either you put these here cuffs on, or I rough you up and put them on. I'm okay if you choose to take the hard way." The sheriff held out the iron wrist cuffs.

"I will do nothing of the sort. Why is that you are so angry and willing to strike out at me? What is it that you don't want to receive the grace and gifts of our Lord and Savior?" The preacher's words began to take the tone of a sermon. He turned to folks who walked the street to stir them up like this wasn't an arrest but a revival. "You!"

A horse hand leading a buck from the stable stopped as the preacher pointed at him. "Me?"

"Yes, you. Are you ready for eternity? Have you accepted God into your life?"

The man looked down at his boots and shook his head no.

"And you…"

Sheriff Flynn clasped an iron on the preacher's wrist when he pointed at a woman. He yanked so the preaching would stop. Silas the Samaritan gritted his teeth and whipped his arm back, and the cuffs flew from Flynn's hand.

"That was a mistake, you fake cuss." Flynn reared back his right hand and stuck that hammer into the left ear of the preacher. Then, another clapped under the evangelist's chin. For most men, that would have been the end of it. But this traveling man of God steadied himself and rubbed his jaw.

The preacher jumped, wrapped his arms around the sheriff, and plowed the lawman into the compact dirt of the street. Like a grizzly, the preacher squeezed the sheriff around his chest.

He stood with Flynn still clasped and squeezed and squeezed. Flynn gasped for air while stuck in the bear hug. With each ratcheted grasp, the sheriff found it harder to breathe and his ribs aching.

The sheriff looked the preacher in the face and clapped both ears of Silas. That was enough. He dropped Flynn.

Flynn tore his pistol from his holster and whipped its butt into the temple of the traveling prophet. That was the end of the fight. Flynn locked the irons on the man with his arms behind his back.

Chapter Four: Brothers No More

Evangeline and Deidre ran out the front door to greet the sheriff as he climbed from his horse. His thick mustache hid a smile right here. Those girls were his light. He snatched them up, one in each arm, and spun them around. Sheriff Flynn gave each one a kiss on the cheek and put them back on the ground. "How's my angels?"

"Good, Uncle Flynn!" they said in unison.

"Your daddy around?" The girls nodded and pointed to the house. Flynn patted each of the blonde girls on their heads. He took a handful of penny candies and poured them into the cupped hands of the young girls. "I need to talk with him, so be good and enjoy your sweets on the porch."

The sheriff's smile disappeared as his boots walked up to the porch and knocked on the screen door. "Ambrose?"

Flynn stood to the side and looked into the house. He could see Ambrose Redd approach the door. "Flynn."

"We need to talk."

"We do? Why's that? I said what I needed to say. I heard what you said. Nothing changed for me. What's changed for you?" Ambrose stepped out on the porch and looked at his girls sitting on the porch, their legs dangling over the edge, mouths full of sugary snacks.

"For starters, Samuel Lee and family, they're dead. And their livestock is gone. I'm going to need to search your barn and farm. Then, you need to know, your preacher friend, he's in my cage, started a fight. And finally, I'm good with you finding religion. I'm just worried whose you found."

"You're holding Silas? For what?" Ambrose straightened up with the question. He kept shaking his head now as his ears got brighter and brighter with color. "He went to town to clear things up."

"If by clear things up, you mean show his hindquarters, he did. He's no good, and I don't want to lose you and the girls to his horse-flop." Flynn looked at the girls enjoying the treats he brought. "Whatever I need to do, I will. You're the closest to kin I got."

"You say that all the time, but family is first and ain't nothing first to your star." Ambrose crossed his arms and turned his back to Flynn. "Girls, let's get inside."

"Hold up. Don't turn your back on me, Ambrose. Girls, sit down." The girls look at each other, confused.

"I didn't ever turn my back on you, Flynn. Not when Daddy got shot, not when you left the line, and not when I moved here, and you followed. I could have turned my back on you any of those times, and the only person who'd've thunk different of me is you."

"And yourself. We stick together, and I know that you think you found some kind of savior, but I'm telling you straight, this man is a devil."

"Yeah, Brother Silas is Satan himself. Listen to you, you don't know. You haven't seen him heal the people who come to him almost dead. I have. I seen him cure Deidre's consumption. You thank him for that?"

Flynn stood silent watching Deidre, mouthful of candy, looking up at her Uncle Flynn.

"No. You accuse him of rustling, being a liar, and fighting in town and lock him up. That man saved my girl. If he says it's God, I believe it. I'd turn my back on anything for my girls. Even if it's a man I called brother the whole of my life."

"Ambrose..."

"You know the farm, walk around. Snoop. You won't find any stolen livestock, but maybe you'll find your sense. When you find that, come calling. Otherwise, next time your boots step on my ground, you'll be wearing them underground." Ambrose walked by Flynn, gathered his daughters, and took them inside.

"Ambrose, brother, don't do this," Flynn spoke through the screen to the back of Ambrose's head.

Ambrose turned and stood for a second. "We're not brothers. Not no more. Do your job, and don't come back."

Flynn shook his head and stepped from the porch. Ever since Silas showed up and convinced Ambrose to join up, he and Flynn had been on the outs. It weighed heavy on the sheriff. He was hard as a coffin nail, but

Ambrose and his family were a soft spot for Sheriff Flynn.

Most folks in town didn't get it, but they were thick from the time they were whelps. Raised together, growed up together, and moved to Sikeston together. Not being friendly with Ambrose was that second problem.

The sheriff did his duty. He walked the farm, checked the barn, and went everywhere he could before the sun started to dip. No stolen cows, no evidence of thieving. In fact, no livestock. As the sheriff expected, even Ambrose's pigs, cows, and goats were absent from the farm. No donkey or even horses.

Where had all those animals gone? Flynn scratched the back of his neck as he walked back from the barn. He could see a lantern burning in the parlor window. No doubt Ambrose and his daughters sat together as he told them stories.

How had this all changed so quickly, and what could be done to stop it? These folks, people Flynn knew, changed almost overnight. And to make things worse,

Ambrose and his farm were at the center of it all. And it seemed the group this Silas attracted grew every time he held a gathering.

Maybe it was time to take a different approach. The frontal attack didn't seem to get the results Flynn wanted. Flynn climbed onto his horse and started back to town.

Chapter 5 – A Tracker Tracks

Flynn let Silas sit in the cell. A few days in there wasn't going to hurt this holy roller. Probably helped him garner some followers. You know how people think. Persecution is reserved for the righteous.

Flynn considered it, cutting the cult leader loose. But the thought of the preacher causing trouble while the sheriff headed to meet up with a tracker he worked with in his days at Fort Smith changed his mind. So, he kept the leader of the Samaritans in lockup. That decision right there, problem number three. The big one.

It was a week that would be burned up, but Flynn didn't have a tracker of any caliber around these parts. He headed out and smiled thinking of the sanctimonious blowhard in a cage. And if the townsfolk hung him in the interim, he'd deal with them, but he'd be happy. Trading a bigger problem for a smaller one.

Either way, it was time to enlist the services of Mad Bear. Mad Bear and Flynn had brought several outlaws to Fort Smith. Saw them swing at the gallows of

Judge Parker and earned enough to cut out their own space in a white man's America.

Mad Bear lived along the banks of Little River. The hunting grounds of his youth as a member of the Osage people. But as America continued her growth, it began to grow, and people came. But Mad Bear still calls the same area home. Now, it goes by Marked Tree, Arkansas.

It took some convincing, but a week later, Flynn rode into town with an Indian beside him. Somehow, the mayor had managed to keep the crowds from stringing up the suspected cattle thief. It didn't hurt that no more cattle was stolen. And people knew when Flynn bothered to say something, he meant it.

In fact, a mob had started to form right after they buried the ashen remainders of the Lee family. But the mayor relayed what Flynn had said. Nope, no one wanted to find private justice after that. No one wanted to stare down their Sikeston Sheriff when he said they'd get the same treatment as the cattle thieves. Flynn came and found his deputies, briefed the mayor on what his plan was, and made sure his friend, Mad Bear, got his fee.

Mad Bear was rightly monikered. He resembled a grizzly, and his constant frown didn't change the mad part none. His black eyes were fearsome, and his skin was a burnt red. His hair was white with streaks of black. He wore a blue cotton shirt, tan leggings, and moccasins that went up to his knees. He spoke only to Flynn, and when the two spoke, it was in the Native's tongue.

All the lawmen of Sikeston rode out to the smoldering charcoal that was once the Lee Farm. Mad Bear sat high in his bone saddle and raised his right arm, signaling for the group of Sheriff Flynn and his four deputies to halt.

The mountain of man, Mad Bear, slid from his horse. He said a few words to Flynn, who then pointed his horse toward the men following him. "Okay, deputies, my friend here, Mad Bear. He needs us to stay put and keep an eye on the road. If you see anyone, pull iron and ride up on them, ready to dispense some justice. He says that there were multiple trips here from the same folks. Be on alert and make sure we all get to climb into our bunks tonight."

The men did as told. Flynn dismounted, and Mad Bear came to him and whispered in his ear. Flynn nodded and watched as the tracker walked the path of the perpetrators.

Mad Bear walked to the blackened timber of the barn and then to the stone foundation that had supported the Lee house. The native began to sing one of them songs that sounded half like crying and half like some banshee.

Mad Bear broke into a sprint, leaped into his saddle, and, with a whoop, kicked the horse's side. Off they shot. Kicking up dust.

"Mount up!" Flynn yelled as he climbed on his trusty steed. And in an instant, the sheriff and deputies cut a swatch of dust as they tried to catch up to Mad Bear. Dust plumed until the Indian took a hard right and cut through a wheat field.

It went on at a breakneck pace for over an hour. The skies grew dark beneath a mass of circling buzzards.

Mad Bear pulled the reins of his horse as he approached a buzzing black cloud and dismounted again.

He covered his mouth as he stood at the edge of a copse of trees. The smell hit the men before they saw what made that foul stink. The smell of death permeated the air, and everyone either pulled their bandanas over their face or cupped their hands over their mouths and noses. It was a graveyard of bovine rotting in the high sun.

The men struggled to keep from being rattled. It was at least two hundred head, rotting on the ground. Flynn pulled out sheets of paper from his saddle while swatting at flies and handed a piece to each deputy. "I know this smells fouler than a latrine in a swamp on a summer day, but these are the brands of the ranches and farms that had their livestock taken. See one that matches, good 'nuff. Cut that swatch of hide and pin the paper to it. You follow?"

The men nodded and fanned out, and one by one, they cut and pulled the brands that matched the brands drawn on their paper. When all the brands had found a match, Sheriff Flynn walked over to Mad Bear, who had made his way out of the cloud of stink and flies.

"Mad Bear, what do you make of this?"

Mad Bear's dark eyes and blank face didn't offer a clue of what tumbled around in his mind. "My friend, I make of this that I want to be back on my land and resting by the river while waiting for the fish to bite. This is a wicked wind washing over your home. It is unnatural. The animals are bloodless, but no one considered to take their meat?"

"What are you talking about? Bloodless?"

"Do you not believe me? Blood pools against the earth when its heart ceases. Roll over a calf and cut it open." Mad Bear bent down and rolled over a young calf and, with a swipe of his Bowie knife, cut the dead animal's underside. He inserted his fingers into the slit and pulled the hide away from the muscle. "No bruising. That means no blood."

"I believe you. But what does that tell you?"

"This is against nature. Evil. We must tread gently." Mad Bear considered his following words. "We have many great journeys together, my old friend. This is the gravest of dangers, and I have seen this day in the dreams of my youth."

"Can you find who left these animals here?"

"I can. I will. And know that I will ever be your friend, and you will not heal the scars cut into you when I find this coyote."

"Law needs serving. I already have the coyote in a cage."

Mad Bear put his hand over Sheriff Flynn's heart. "You and Mad Bear, we are brothers. I do this because it is as it should be. Send your men back to town to keep the coyote in its cage."

Flynn nodded and made his way to his men, who were busy trying to keep the flies from themselves and their horses. He started in Siouan, then corrected himself and switched to English. "Mad Bear and I will follow the trail to whoever stole these animals. I need you all to go back to the jail and make sure no one gets to this sidewinding hornswoggling preacher. When I get back, be ready to round up his followers."

Flynn pulled the bandana from his nose as he watched his men disappear on their way back to town. Mad Bear walked behind him and placed his hand on the sheriff's back. "My brother, are you ready to walk this path?"

"Born ready." Flynn sauntered over to his horse and took the reins. "Lead the way."

"Be ready." Mad Bear climbed into the saddle, and the two began to head through the circle of trees in front of the dead animals. The buzzing of the flies and stench grew weaker as they moved through a small wooded area.

As they left the woods, Flynn near fell out of his saddle. "Well, I'll be cussed. This is Ambrose's farm! I should have recognized where we were, damn."

"Your other brother?" Mad Bear sighed and shook his head. "He has placed his lot with a great evil. They live on the edge of the west."

"West? We're heading east. You talking that medicine man stuff? Mad Bear, you know I don't find much value in any such talk."

"Does not matter. It is true." Mad Bear shifted in the saddle to look his riding partner in the eye. "When this is done, never forget it is your lot to pay for a brother with a brother."

"Fine. Can we just get this over with?"

"As you ask, I finish my journey, and yours will continue."

"Stop that talk, arm yourself. If Ambrose is here, this isn't going down easy." Flynn pulled his repeater rifle from its holster on the saddle. Mad Bear pulled out his antler-handled Bowie knife and clinched it in his teeth while he took his pistol from its holster.

The two got down from their horses and tethered them to the trees. Hunched down, the two old warriors approached the house, ready to open fire. Flynn couldn't hide his disappointment as he looked into the house and walked right in the back door to no resistance. In fact, the house was empty.

"Don't worry, Brother. The fight is coming." Mad Bear pointed to a few men in the open doors of the barn. "Shoot them now?"

"I'm the law. That'd be cold-blooded murder and awful yella of me." Flynn did raise his rifle and sight in on all three of the men. They looked to be busy with something.

"It would. I would definitely think less of you," Mad Bear said with a smile.

"We walk out the front door, guns raised, ready to fire. Walk up to them and sort it out there." Flynn tilted his head as if his sentence was a question.

"We should do that, Brother." Mad Bear opened the door, walked out onto the porch, and straight toward the men. The men in the barn continued working. Flynn stepped out behind him. Mad Bear had already covered half the span to the men in the barn.

Flynn ran after his friend. But the people in the barn saw Mad Bear first. One of the men began to walk toward the approaching Indian. He held a small ax wet with blood. "Who are you?"

"I am Mad Bear. I was hired by the Sheriff Flynn. We come to take you to your justice."

"Hey, boys, you hear the heathen? He's here to take us to justice."

The two other men stood. One held a rip saw and the other a cleaver. The one with the saw said, "That right?"

The other with cleaver said, "Are you Jesus? Because that's whose work we're about. We are Samaritans, and we aim to heal the sick, help the lost, and serve our God."

"You are cattle thieves and sick-minded fools. Drop them tools, and I won't shoot you!" Sheriff Flynn leaned his cheek against his rifle to make sure his first shot would send the message if they didn't listen.

"You are welcome to join us, sheriff. All are welcome in the house of the Lord. Stop serving the world, join the Samaritans, and serve the kingdom of God." The man with the ax said.

"How about we discuss this in town? Put down your weapons," Sheriff Flynn instructed. But they weren't in a listening mood. Mad Bear continued to walk toward them. "Mad Bear, stay back."

"No, Brother." Mad Bear holstered his pistol in favor of his Bowie knife. "I can see what they are doing. Shoot."

Flynn didn't ask questions. His trigger finger squeezed. The man with the ax dropped to the ground beneath the red mist that exploded from his forehead.

Mad Bear let out a whoop as he rushed at the other two men. Flynn cocked the lever of his rifle. The next round dropped the man with the saw. Mad Bear's knife split the chest of the man with the cleaver open.

Mad Bear went down as the man collapsed and shoved his Bowie knife to the hilt. Flynn rushed down to Mad Bear. The massive Indian struggled to pull his blade from the man. He freed it and stood. His eyes grew big. "Brother, behind you!"

The man with an ax stood with a hole in his forehead. Blood gushed from the bullet's entry point. With a roar, he ran at Flynn, who dropped his attacker with three rapid rounds from his rifle. "He had a hole in his head! How could he get up from that?"

"Brother, I told you, I dreamt this. I saw this years ago." Mad Bear put his hand over his heart, "Brother for a brother. May you find your way east."

Meat cleaver crushed through the old Indian's skull. A single line of blood crept from Mad Bear's white hair, rolled down the center of his face, and dripped from his nose to the ground. The man with the cleaver then bit into the Indian's neck. Flynn took the opportunity to blow a hole in his head. The man fell back. The man with the saw stood up, and Flynn again fired. And again. He heard a rustling behind him.

All three of the men that should be dead stood, and they circled around the sheriff of Sikeston.

Chapter Six – An Escape From An Angry Mob

The deputies rode into town ready to keep the cattle-stealing, serpent-tongued evangelist in lockup and prepared to fight his followers. They weren't ready to fight a group of Satanic Samaritans waiting for them imbued with supernatural strength.

Ambrose Redd shot three of their horses as the thirty or so Samaritans, blood-covered and possessed by evil, charged the other two. They pulled the men, who fired their revolvers at the Samaritans, from their mounts.

The horses reared up, beating at the attackers with their front hooves. Then, the screams began. As the demon enthralled mass of worshippers began to rend the doomed riders limb from trunk.

It was those screams that had the townsfolk streaming out to see what caused such a calamitous cacophony. Women fainted dead away. But the men gasped. Some with yellow streaks ran back to where they came from. Others went and fetched the nearest object they could use as a weapon. Those thusly armed opened fire on the mass of crazed zealots.

Ambrose stood on the porch of the jail, shielding the offending preacher from the hail of gunfire. He aimed well and picked off the best shots among the townsfolk with his true aim.

Instead of getting the people of Sikeston to back down, it riled them up like an angry bunch of hornets with someone poking at their nest.

"Ambrose, we must make our way back to your farm," Silas the preacher, said.

"I'm fixing to. But I'm not sure we can find a way out of this!" Ambrose said. He worked to reload his revolver. The crazed Samaritans, faces red with the blood of the deputies, formed a line between the growing mob and Ambrose Redd and the head Samaritan, Silas.

"Is that better?" Silas asked. He then stepped to the edge of the porch. "People of Sikeston, I have walked among you, and God has found you wanting. Only a few of you have taken on the boon of the power of His blood, and for that, you fall under the curse of original sin. As God judged Adam, so has he judged you. You will perish. You can choose to do so today and rush to your judgment, or you can hope to find a way to correct your path and perish on another day. The choice is yours, but this day, God is on the side of the Samaritans."

"You ain't no man of God!" One of the townspeople shouted from the still-growing mob.

"I am, but as Jesus returned to Nazareth and found those people faithless, I have found the same in Sikeston. Let us leave in peace, and you will delay your judgment until you stand before the Bema seat and your maker. Or.."

"You stole cattle and killed our deputies. That ain't no Godly man's way!" The crowd agreed. And with the comment, the group began to advance. The line of Samaritans stood fast.

"Or you meet your maker today. We will leave peaceably, or we will spill the covenant of your precious blood into the dust of Sikeston's streets." Silas stepped into the street and through the line of his followers. "The invitation still stands for you all to join the ranks of the Samaritans and follow me to Beulah Land."

"Get out of our town!" The mayor pushed to the front. He then faced the angry crowd. "Stand down. If they are leaving, let them leave. I don't want any more of you hurt."

The crowd murmured and talked among themselves. "They stole our cattle, and look what they did to our deputies!"

"You're not the law. And you need to let the law handle this. We aren't savages. We are civilized people." The mayor tried his level best to calm the crowd. To stall them until Flynn showed up. "Our sheriff never failed us before, and he's not going to start now. Let the wheels of justice turn as we all deserve. Trust in the process."

Silas smiled. He wasn't going to wait for a more significant sign. He began to walk away from the crowd, and his followers took his example. Ambrose became the scorpion tail of the line of Samaritans. He held his stinger at the ready, to sink it's lead poison to anyone with foolish ideas.

The mob began to administer care to the deputies who cooled in the streets of the town they served. Their sacrifice was met with sadness and anger. Flames of private justice were fanned. And soon, there would be little the mayor could do to hold back the vigilante impulses. Even if Flynn appeared in short time.

Mayor Shelby pulled the tin stars from the dead men in the street. "Sikeston needs men ready to serve the law and mete out justice. I need twenty. When Flynn comes back..." The mayor pulled his watch from his pocket. He pursed his lips and blew out a stream of air. "If he comes back, we need to be ready to roll out and dispense justice and purge these rabble rousers from our community."

One by one, the bravest stepped forward. All ages, from young sturdy saplings to broad aged oaks. Solid men ready to protect their homes and their neighbors. The mayor called forward five of these brave men: Jim Bridger, Samuel Hall, Robert Gunn, Hubert Brom, and Edgar Irving. They all served in the Great Rebellion. Some for the Union and others for the Rebels.

But here and now, they all stood for their chosen home, Sikeston, Missouri.

Chapter Seven – Burying a Brother & 3 Hanged

The sun sat at the horizon behind the silhouette of a man walking two horses. Hues of orange to deep blue stretched from the earth to the heavens. The cowboy's head hung low as he led the mares onto the streets of Sikeston. The horses nickered as their journey for the day was at its end, rode hard, and now laden with a burden.

On each horse were the bodies of two men. Sheriff Flynn's eyes, watery to the point of leaking, looked down Front Street to his cabin. Home hurt today. He came out on top, but not without it costing him. He could see that lazy old walrus of a politician sitting in his rocker. Flynn exhaled. He was too tired to offer even anger.

"Mayor."

The mayor stopped rocking and popped up from the chair. "Thank God. Sheriff Flynn, I feared the worst."

"Well, I don't go down easy. What's got you on my porch and not home with Sarah or up in the Central with a whore?" Sheriff Flynn didn't want to mince words. He sought to get his friend to the undertaker and then string up four, the three Samaritans he brought back to town and that darned pastor. "I got work to do still, so spill it, plain as you can."

"That cattle-thieving, murdering preacher, his zealots broke him out." The mayor waited for a breath to share the rest. "They killed your deputies."

Sheriff Flynn pulled his hat from his head and struck Mayor Shelby with it. "Useless. That's you."

"Flynn, I tried, but Ambrose shot your two best men and then started gunning down people in the street." The mayor lowered his head, "This is the darkest day of my mayorship. I let you down, and I let the people of Sikeston down."

"That you did. But what're going to do about that?" Flynn pulled at the thick hair of his mustache.

"I got twenty men ready to ride out with us. To take those vile Samaritans down."

"Do you?"

"I deputized the best of them. They are waiting for you at the saloon."

"Well, they will wait a bit longer. I got some business to tend to." Flynn put his hat back on and gave a square look into the mayor's eyes, "You said us. Are you ready to ride? It's going to be a bloodbath."

"I'm ready for a rampage."

"Right then. I will circle back after I gather the posse. Be ready." Flynn continued to the undertaker. There, he purchased the finest casket for Mad Bear. Left instructions for the undertaker to take Mad Bear back to his home in Marked Tree. He handed over several gold coins. It was good to know that Mad Bear would rest by the riverside.

Flynn stormed into the bar, "Mayor Shelby says I can find men here."

The whole saloon stood and cheered. And one by one the men of Sikeston shook the sheriff's hand. He sorted them out as he met them. Which would lead, which would hang back, and which he'd leave in town, you know, to protect it. He divided the room of now fifty men into those groups. He would ride out with fifteen men plus the five the mayor gave tin stars to.

The remaining men, Mayor Shelby among them, Flynn gave them places to stand watch in shifts. He dispatched them before gathering the twenty who would ride out.

Flynn told them what to expect and what he needed each of them to do. Sheriff Flynn's primary concern was the safe recovery of the two young daughters of Ambrose, Deidre and Evangeline. After escorting the young women to safety, they would round up the Samaritans and bring them to justice.

But first, it was time to send a message. Flynn was exhausted, fueled only by a grief-stricken rage. The men gathered rope from the livery while Flynn guided the horses with the three Samaritans on their backs to the last light posts on the edge of town.

Flynn wanted to be surprised when they groaned and moved. He wasn't. He just hit them with the butt of his rifle. Cussed them. When they didn't stop struggling, Flynn flipped them off the horses, sending them thudding on the compact ground. After a few kicks and three more rounds from his Spencer Repeater, the squirming ceased.

The men selected to ride out to the Redd Ranch came with several lengths of rope. Flynn kicked a Samaritan and said, "You all want to wiggle? Time to string you murdering, thieving pest up. Fix up three nooses."

The men tied nooses, and one by one, the Samaritans that killed Mad Bear were hoisted on the lamp posts that entered the town on the west end. The hanging men jerked and twisted. Flynn stopped that by wrapping his arms around their knees and giving a sharp tug, breaking their necks.

Flynn was satisfied work was done in town. Flynn smiled and thought of his friend Mad Bear. The debt was paid when the rest of the Samaritans swung with these three. Flynn directed his new deputies. He barked, "All right. Let's round up our horses. Get some torches and lanterns, and we ride out to Redd Ranch!"

Chapter Eight – Sheriff Flynn Fights Satan Himself

Flynn's back was tight, and his muscles were sore as he pushed through the pain to finish the job. The men galloped through the dark night by lantern light. No doubt they would be seen, but this wasn't a numbers game, and Flynn would stop only if he died. Vengeance and justice mixed in his scarred heart, and tonight, he planned to drink from that cup.

The windows in the house grinned with malice at the men with the pale light within. No doubt, the Samaritans waited within, ready for the law and his posse to show up. Ambrose knew Flynn well enough and would have them prepared for the fight. Flynn and his men slid from the backs of their horses and readied their weapons. Cocked, loaded, and aimed, the twenty-one men advanced.

Flynn ordered the men to spread out and cover him as he headed up to the door. The steps creaked with each footfall. He peered through the glass in the door. He could see the flicker of the lantern light in the empty room. With a hand signal, he told the men to stay. Tremors began as his hand reached for the handle. Twisting the knob, the latch clanked from its rest, and the door groaned as it swung outward.

Flynn poked his head inside. Empty Parlor and dining room. He stepped inside and, gun at the ready, crept through the empty front of the house. The click of his heel sounded like a kettledrum as his senses heightened. Flynn's eyes darted around the room. He slowed his breathing. The hairs on his arms rose. He pressed his back against the hall wall. The sheriff inched his way to the back of the house toward the kitchen.

The door was closed. His jittery hand reached to push the door open, and he aimed his Colt Model 1862. Ready to shoot anything on the other side. The door swung open and back. In the brief swing of the door, he saw the room barren of enemies.

Where were the girls? Flynn took a breath, his lips smacked as he drew them apart. "Deidre? Evangeline? Uncle Flynn is here to get you somewhere safe."

The kitchen door smashed into the back of the sheriff. Crashed to his knees, Flynn's Colt rattled and slid away on the rough pine floors. Flynn rolled onto his back to put eyes on whoever pushed the door.

With a blood-covered face, Ambrose rumbled toward the sheriff from the kitchen. The blade flashed as it sunk into the sheriff's shoulder as Flynn tried to regain his footing. The burning sting of the steel slipping into the meat of his shoulder didn't dominate his senses long. Ambrose was on him.

The sheriff raised his arm to shield the attack. Ambrose's hands grabbed at Flynn's head and exposed his neck. Flynn could feel the hot iron breath of Ambrose straining for his neck. Flynn tried again to push Ambrose from him. Ambrose reared his head back and sunk his teeth into the sheriff's arm. Flynn screamed as Ambrose's jaws clenched and his teeth cut through his cotton sleeve and the flesh beneath.

With all his strength, Flynn pulled to free his arm from the bite of Ambrose. A chunk of his arm ripped off into Ambrose's mouth. Blood gushed from the massive piece gone from this arm. Flynn kicked his assailant off him and slid to his revolver.

Without a thought, he emptied the six-shooter into the chest of Ambrose Redd. He could see the back of the house through the hole he shot into the center of Ambrose's chest.

Blood spurted from the mouth of Ambrose. His eyes were big, like a full moon over an open prairie. His hand reached out for Flynn. Once like brothers, the two men found themselves in a mortal toil. "Consarn it, Ambrose. This is zactly what I didn't want. You're my only family."

Flynn crawled over to his fallen blood brother and held him until he was still. The men who rode out to the ranch stood silently at the door and watched the surly sheriff cross the arms on the lifeless body of Ambrose Redd and, with two fingers, close the dead man's eyes.

Flynn stood, reloaded. He looked at Ambrose, holding back all the emotion swirling inside, and said, "Brother for a brother. You can rest, Mad Bear. But I am damned."

Flynn was shocked to see the men he rode in with standing silent. They nodded. "He's the only one in the house, and he was my brother. He's dead because of that cursed preacher and his pack of lies. Let's find that son of a whore and stretch his holy neck. Make sure the girls are safe before just shooting things up. There are another twenty or thirty Samaritans who walked out of town today. Keep a keen eye out, and let's rampage over these Satanic bastards."

The men followed Flynn, who grabbed his Spencer Repeater from his horse, up to the barn. Ready to blaze up the night in a hail of gunfire. Screams of horror filled the night. The grief of killing a brother vanished. Anger replaced the sadness that Flynn could not kill his "brother" again.

The two girls hung from the rafters of the barn as God brought them into the world. They were dressed and prepared as if a butcher went to work on them.

Flynn cussed and wept as he cut them free of the ropes. He cradled them and sang a lullaby as the tears fell on their cold, white flesh. The men, dismayed and enraged, went out searching for signs of the preacher or the Samaritans. Only a few stayed with Flynn.

The grieving was short. Something rattled in the back of the barn. A large shadow stepped into the lantern light. A devilish black form that sucked the light from the flames lighting the barn. Flynn jumped to his feet. He cocked his rifle and fired shot after shot until it dry-fired. He then pulled his pistol, and all the men came running.

The thing laughed as twenty-one men emptied every round into the dark, hulking form. The barn filled with gunsmoke. The men could no longer see or hear the laughter. When the smoke cleared, the barn was empty. But the men's hearts filled with fear. They stood together, watching for anything moving in the dark.

The sun came, and it was clear that the devil from the barn was gone. And that he took the Satanic Samaritans with him. Sheriff Flynn and his deputies were left to bury the dead and live with a mystery that would trouble them for the remainder of their days. Disturbed by what evils they saw. Haunted that they fought the devil to a draw and that the devil stole from the good folks of Sikeston.

And worst of all, that third problem, is that no justice could be had.

The End?

You rode out to fight the Satanic Samaritans.
And You Were Surly Enough to Survive the
Rampage at Redd Ranch
with Sheriff Flynn!

But wait, the thrills and chills aren't over.
Get ready to journey deeper into the unknown
with another FREE book.

Your Adventure Continues!
Unveil More Mysteries!

Head to www.danielbautzctp.com
and claim your FREE copy of
The Haunting of McMurtry Manor,
a psychical investigation of a cursed
and haunted mansion with Brannigan Rafferty.

Ready for more?
Venture to Amazon.com to uncover the companion piece,
Life Is In The Blood,
where Brannigan Rafferty and Sheriff Flynn's
destinies entwine, revealing secrets
you won't want to miss.

Your next adventure awaits.
Will you answer the call?

ABOUT THE AUTHOR

Daniel Bautz's journey to become a chilling, thrilling author of horror adventure began in rural Ohio. His artistic origins started with his grandma teaching him to paint and inheriting drawing skills from his grandfather. While earning a living in graphic design, he attempted filmmaking with mixed success. The foray into filmmaking helped him to realize his true creative calling lay in writing.

Despite hosting a podcast and pursuing filmmaking, writing emerged as his passion. With the guidance of his brother, he refined his storytelling abilities. In 2022, he signed with Anatolian Press. In 2023, he achieved a significant milestone by releasing his award-winning debut novel "Life Is In The Blood," now followed by "Aristotle James and the Phantom Funeral Coach," cementing his transformation from an aspiring artist to a published author.

Don't miss out and stay current on
Daniel Bautz by visiting DanielBautzCTP.com
and subscribing to his newsletter.

In Millersburg, Ohio, Silas Hemfant's mission is to turn the community to the Lord. His business? Feasting on their blood and adding to his immortal legion.

Miriam, devout and torn by faith's hidden truths, is drawn to an enigmatic prophet. Brannigan, a famous author, couldn't care less about truth; he just wants to sell books. Flynn, a skilled lawman, is driven by vengeance and past failures.

Three strangers, each with their own path, are mysteriously drawn to a small Ohio town. A force compels them to confront good and evil. But what if the greatest evil masquerades as virtue?

Irresistible Call to Action:
"Life is in the Blood" is an unmissable journey into longing, freedom, love, and the essence of humanity. Don't miss this captivating tale.

What darkness lies hidden within the walls of McMurtry Manor? Discover Brannigan Rafferty's "The Haunting of McMurtry Manor," a chilling prequel set just before the blood-curdling "Life Is In The Blood."

Dear reader, are you brave enough to confront the chilling secrets hidden within the manor's walls? Unearth the malevolent past and plunge into a black world that devours hope in a quest to find the answers that haunt us all.

Step into McMurtry Manor and dare to face the unspeakable evil that resides within. Feel the relentless pursuit of answers as you follow Brannigan Rafferty, America's foremost psychical researcher.

DO YOU BELIEVE IN GHOSTS?

It's 1987, and what starts as a regular scout trip transforms into a pulse-pounding quest for Aristotle and AJ.

Get ready for an adventure that will send shivers down your spine! Join 12-year-old Aristotle James and his trusty sidekick, AJ, his best friend and Siberian husky, on a heart-pounding journey through the eerie town of Lucas, Ohio. At every step, Aristotle and AJ put their bravery to the test. But Courage knows no age limits. And Aristotle and AJ aren't your typical heroes.

They're on a mission to save their town from an ancient evil, and they're not backing down. Armed with friendship, they confront the unknown and unearth truths that send spine-tingling chills down your back.

A Collection of lost and found from the orphanage of forsaken stories. An eclectic group of 22 stories that offer more than one genre. Sometimes scary, sometimes uplifting, sometimes funny, but never dull. From angels to demons, Halloween to Christmas, from endings to new beginnings, every story gives the reader something different than the last.

Christmas is under attack, and John Trafalgar, the Santa Claus serving the United States, finds himself caught in the crossfire.

He must fight his way from captivity and find his way back to the North Pole before December 25th while protecting the secrets of his adopted home. Using the combat techniques he learned in special ops in Nam, his wits, and help from the Saints of Nicholas, this is one Santa who's not going down easy.

With December 25 coming up fast, time is running out. The secret government organization on his trail will stop at nothing to keep him from saving Christmas. John Trafalgar, aka Santa Claus, and Christmas are in real trouble. The War on Christmas is heating up and Santa is coming Down The Chimney!

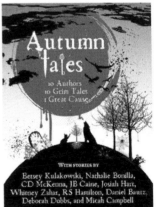

Autumn Tales is a different kind of anthology. It is a horror anthology with heart.

It is a horrifying collection of ghastly tales told by some of the most influential new authors in paranormal and horror. In Autumn Tales, the authors use the needle of words and the thread of fear to stitch a tapestry so dark it shadows every nightmare you ever had.

All royalties from Amazon orders are going to help endangered children! The authors are donating 100% of royalties made from Amazon purchases to Collective Liberty, a non-profit organization that is in the trenches of the battle against Human Trafficking!

37893914R00041